30 BEDTIME STORIES FOR 30 DIFFERENT NIGHTS

vol. 1

Marc Sala López

To my wife and kids for their love and support.

CONTENTS

THE GLOBAL POTLUCK DINNER

Once upon a time, in a colorful and bustling neighborhood where every house looked different and every garden bloomed with unique flowers, the people decided to have a very special dinner. They wanted to celebrate their friendship and learn more about each other, so they organized a Global Potluck Dinner. This wasn't just any dinner; it was a magical evening where every family would bring a dish from their culture to share.

As the sun began to dip below the horizon, painting the sky in shades of orange and pink, the community park started to fill with the delicious smells of foods from all over the world. Tables were draped in cloths as colorful as a rainbow, and lanterns hung from the trees like twinkling stars.

The first to arrive was the Garcia family, carrying a big pot of Paella, a rice dish bursting with seafood and a rich saffron aroma from Spain. They set their pot down on the table, and little Maria excitedly explained to her friends how her abuela taught her to sprinkle the spices just right.

Next came the Patel family, with a large, steaming tray of Samosas, filled with spiced potatoes and peas, a favorite snack in India. Anaya Patel, with a smile as warm as the spices in her samosas, shared how her family makes them together during festivals, folding the dough into perfect triangles.

Then, the Nguyen family arrived, bringing with them the fresh and vibrant flavors of Vietnam with a platter of Spring Rolls. Wrapped in thin rice paper, these rolls were packed with vegetables, noodles, and shrimp, served with a tangy dipping sauce. Linh Nguyen, only four years old, giggled as she showed her friends how to dip the rolls without dripping sauce on their clothes.

The Johnson family, originally from the United States, didn't want to be left out. They brought a classic American barbecue dish—slow-cooked, tender Pulled Pork sandwiches. James Johnson, who loved to help his dad grill, told everyone about the secret ingredient in their barbecue sauce: a dash of apple cider vinegar for an extra zing.

From Italy, the Rossi family brought a large, mouth-watering Lasagna, layered with cheese, tomato sauce, and ground meat. Little Sofia Rossi beamed with pride as she described helping her nonna layer the pasta and spread the rich, creamy cheese.

The dessert table was a sight to behold. The O'Connor family from Ireland brought a tray of warm, buttery Scones, served with jam and cream. Meanwhile, the Mbeki family from South Africa added a colorful touch with their Koeksisters, syrupy twisted doughnuts that were sticky and sweet.

As the evening went on, the park buzzed with laughter and music. Children ran around playing tag, their faces painted with joy and, occasionally, a bit of sauce. Parents exchanged recipes and stories of their homelands, their ancestors, and the journeys that brought them to this neighborhood.

The highlight of the evening was the storytelling corner, where grandparents shared tales from their countries, enchanting the children with stories of brave heroes, clever animals, and magical lands far away. The children sat, wide-eyed, as they traveled the world through these stories, learning that even though their friends might come from different places, they shared many of the same dreams and joys.

As the moon climbed high into the night sky, casting a soft glow over the park, everyone gathered for a final moment. Holding hands in a large circle, they shared what they were thankful for. Each person, from the smallest child to the oldest grandparent, expressed gratitude for the community, the food, and the new friendships that had grown stronger that night.

The Global Potluck Dinner became a cherished tradition in the neighborhood, a night to celebrate the diversity that made their community so special. It taught them that sharing a meal was more than just eating; it was a way of coming together, learning from each other, and creating a bond that no distance or difference could break.

As the families said their goodbyes, the children, tired but happy, promised to meet the next day to play and perhaps, share another meal. Because in this neighborhood, every day was an opportunity to learn something new and celebrate the beautiful tapestry of cultures that made up their world.

And so, under the starlit sky, the park slowly emptied, left with only the echoes of laughter and the lingering scents of a meal that had brought the world together, if only for an evening. The Global Potluck Dinner was more than just a dinner; it was a reminder of the joy of sharing, the beauty of diversity, and the magic of friendship that knew no borders.

The End.

ADVENTURES IN ANCIENT CHINA

Once upon a time, in a land filled with rolling hills, majestic mountains, and vast rivers, there was a magical kingdom known as Ancient China. This land was unlike any other, with secrets and wonders waiting to be discovered by two curious children, Mei and Lin.

Mei, with her bright eyes and adventurous spirit, and Lin, with his clever mind and boundless curiosity, were the best of friends. One sunny morning, they stumbled upon an ancient map, hidden in an old chest in their grandmother's attic. The map was adorned with dragons and phoenixes, and at its center was a drawing of the Great Wall, so long it seemed to stretch into infinity.

Excited by their find, Mei and Lin decided to embark on an adventure to explore the wonders of Ancient China. Their first stop was, of course, the Great Wall. With a whoosh of magic from the ancient map, they found themselves standing before the colossal structure. It was more magnificent than they could have imagined, with its stones stretching up and down across the landscape, as far as their eyes could see.

"The Great Wall was built by the people of China to protect their land," Mei said, remembering the stories their grandmother told them.

As they walked along the wall, they marveled at its strength and the effort it must have taken to build such an enormous barrier. They imagined the soldiers of ancient times, guarding the kingdom from atop the wall, brave and vigilant.

Their adventure continued as the map led them to a mysterious workshop, filled with inventions centuries ahead of their time. Here, they discovered the compass, which sailors used to navigate the vast oceans. They also found paper, so thin and light, and yet strong enough to carry the words of wisdom and poetry. And there was the printing press, which allowed people to share knowledge far and wide.

"Wow, the people of Ancient China were so clever!" Lin exclaimed, his eyes wide with wonder.

Next, the ancient map whisked Mei and Lin away to a beautiful palace, home to the emperors of the Chinese dynasties. They learned about the Han Dynasty, when the Silk Road opened and connected China to the rest of the world. They visited the Tang Dynasty, a golden age of art and culture, where poets wrote beautiful verses under the moonlit sky.

In each dynasty, Mei and Lin met kind and wise rulers who taught them about the importance of harmony, the beauty of nature, and the value of learning and innovation. They saw gardens with pavilions and bridges over koi ponds, and they tasted delicious foods like mooncakes and dumplings, each with its own story.

As the day turned into night, the stars above Ancient China began to twinkle, reminding Mei and Lin that it was time to return home. With a heavy heart, they said goodbye to the friends they had made and the wonders they had seen. The ancient map glowed one last time, and in the blink of an eye, they were back in their grandmother's attic.

Sitting among the treasures of the past, Mei and Lin couldn't help but feel changed by their journey. They had walked the Great Wall, marveled at ancient inventions, and learned the rich history of the Chinese dynasties. But more importantly, they discovered the spirit of curiosity and the joy of exploration.

As they put the ancient map back into the old chest, they made a promise to never forget the adventures they had in Ancient China. They knew that the world was full of wonders waiting to be explored, and this was just the beginning of their journeys.

That night, as Mei and Lin fell asleep, their dreams were filled with dragons soaring through the sky, emperors sharing ancient wisdom, and the Great Wall standing tall and proud, a symbol of the enduring spirit of discovery and adventure.

And so, the story of Mei and Lin's adventures in Ancient China became a cherished tale, passed down through generations, inspiring children everywhere to explore the world with open hearts and curious minds.

The End.

THE SYMPHONY OF THE FOREST

Once upon a time, in a lush, green forest filled with tall trees and hidden trails, there was a secret that only came alive as the sun dipped below the horizon and the moon took its place in the sky. This secret was not a creature, nor a hidden treasure, but a magical event known as "The Symphony of the Forest."

As daylight faded, the little creatures of the forest began to stir. The first to wake were the crickets, tuning their tiny instruments as the stars blinked open in the night sky. Their music started softly, a gentle chirping that whispered through the leaves.

Next to join the symphony were the owls, perched high in the treetops. They hooted in harmony, adding a deep, soothing melody that echoed far and wide. Their wise eyes watched over the forest, conducting the music with the flap of their wings.

Then, from the babbling brooks and streams, came the frogs. They croaked and ribbited with joy, their voices bubbling up like laughter. Their song was playful and merry, making the water dance and sparkle under the moonlight.

Not wanting to be left out, the fireflies added their light to the symphony. They blinked on and off, creating a visual rhythm that matched the music. Their tiny lights looked like stars that had descended to join the celebration, twinkling in the darkness.

The rustling leaves joined in too, as the gentle night breeze played them like a harp. Each leaf fluttered and swayed, adding a soft, rustling percussion to the symphony. The trees themselves seemed to sway in time with the music, their branches conducting the orchestra of the night.

Even the night flowers contributed to the symphony. They opened their petals wide, releasing sweet fragrances that wafted through the air, adding a sensory depth to the music that could be felt in the heart and soul.

As the night deepened, the symphony reached its crescendo. Every creature, big and small, joined in. The forest was alive with sound, a beautiful, harmonious blend of life and music. It was a celebration of the ecosystem, a reminder of how every living thing, no matter how small, contributes to the beauty of the world.

But the most magical part of the Symphony of the Forest was yet to come. For at the very peak of the night, when the music was at its most beautiful, the Great Old Tree, the oldest and wisest tree in the forest, began to sing. Its deep, resonant voice was like nothing else in the forest. It sang of ancient times, of the cycles of life, and of the deep, unbreakable connections between all living things.

The creatures of the forest listened in awe, feeling a deep sense of peace and unity. The Great Old Tree's song was a reminder that they were all part of something bigger, a vast, interconnected web of life that thrived in harmony.

As dawn approached, the symphony gradually quieted down. The creatures, tired but happy, returned to their homes, snuggling into their nests and burrows, or settling onto their perches and branches. The forest fell silent once more, but the magic of the night lingered in the air, a sweet memory that would stay with them until the next symphony began.

And so, night after night, the Symphony of the Forest played on, a never-ending celebration of the music of nature. It was a secret that belonged to the forest, a magical experience that taught the creatures about the beauty of their ecosystem and the importance of living in harmony.

The End.

THE ENCHANTED BOOK OF SPELLS

Once upon a time, in a cozy little town nestled between the whispering forests and the sparkling rivers, there lived a curious little girl named Lily and her adventurous little brother, Alex. Their days were filled with laughter, play, and endless wonder about the world around them. But one day, their grandpa, a wise old man with twinkling eyes and a gentle smile, brought them a gift unlike any other—a thick, ancient book bound in shimmering emerald leather, titled "The Enchanted Book of Spells."

Grandpa said, "This is no ordinary book. It holds the secrets of the world, the magic of nature, and the wisdom of the ages. But remember, with great power comes great responsibility. Use it wisely, and it will guide you on incredible adventures."

Lily and Alex's eyes widened with excitement. That night, under the soft glow of their bedroom lamp, they opened the book for the first time. The pages seemed to come alive, glowing softly, each word dancing before their eyes. The first spell they found was "The Whisper of the Wind." The book taught them to listen to the wind, to understand its stories, and to respect the secrets it carried from faraway lands.

With eager hearts, they whispered the spell, and a gentle breeze filled their room, whispering tales of distant mountains and deep, blue seas. They learned about the birds that soared across the skies and the trees that stood tall and proud, guardians of the earth. The wind taught them the importance of listening, of being kind to nature, and of the interconnectedness of all things.

The next day, guided by the enchanted book, Lily and Alex discovered the "Dance of the Rain." This spell taught them to feel the rhythm of the raindrops, to see the beauty in the storms, and to understand the rain's role in bringing life to the earth. As they chanted the spell, soft raindrops began to tap against their window, inviting them to dance in its melody. They learned the value of water, the joy of growth, and the cycle of life.

Each day, the book revealed a new spell, a new adventure. There was the "Gleam of the Moon," which taught them about the mysteries of the night, the stars' stories, and the dreams that come alive under the moonlight. They learned to look up in wonder, to dream big, and to believe in the magic within them.

But with each spell they learned, Grandpa reminded them, "Remember, the greatest power lies not in the spells themselves, but in the knowledge and wisdom they bring. Use them to make the world a better place, to spread kindness, and to help others."

One evening, as a storm raged outside, the town's river began to rise, threatening to flood the little town. Remembering the "Dance of the Rain," Lily and Alex knew what they had to do. They opened the enchanted book and, with brave hearts, chanted the spell, not to dance with the rain this time, but to ask it to be gentle, to spare their town.

The rain listened. It slowed to a gentle drizzle, and the river's rise halted, saving the town from the flood. The townspeople, amazed and grateful, gathered around Lily and Alex, thanking them for their courage and wisdom.

From that day on, Lily and Alex were known not just as the children who had saved the town, but as the keepers of knowledge, the young wizards who understood the true power of the enchanted book. They continued to learn from the book, to go on adventures, and to share the wisdom they gained with others.

And so, "The Enchanted Book of Spells" taught them, and all who heard their story, that knowledge is the greatest magic of all, a treasure to be shared with kindness and responsibility. And as long as they remembered this, the magic of the book would live on forever, in their hearts, and in the heart of the world.

The End.

EXPLORING THE
EXOPLANETS

Once upon a time, in a cozy little town under the vast, twinkling sky, lived a curious child named Alex. Alex loved to gaze at the stars every night, dreaming about the mysteries they held. One evening, while Alex was looking up at the sky, a shimmering, silver spaceship appeared out of nowhere! It landed gently in Alex's backyard, and out stepped a friendly robot named Luna.

"Luna!" exclaimed Alex, wide-eyed with wonder. "Are you from space?"

"Yes, Alex," Luna replied with a smile. "And I've come to take you on an adventure across the universe to explore the exoplanets!"

"Exoplanets? What are those?" asked Alex, bouncing with excitement.

"Exoplanets are planets that orbit stars outside our solar system. There are so many of them, each unique and full of surprises. Are you ready to explore some with me?" Luna extended a shiny, metallic hand.

Alex nodded eagerly, and together, they boarded the spaceship. With a whoosh, they zoomed off into the night sky, leaving the Earth far behind. Their first destination was Gliese 667 Cc, a rocky exoplanet orbiting a red dwarf star.

As they landed on Gliese 667 Cc, Alex noticed the sky was a beautiful shade of orange. "This planet is in the habitable zone, where it's not too hot and not too cold, perfect for water to exist in liquid form," explained Luna.

"Could there be life here?" Alex asked, looking around curiously.

"It's possible," Luna said. "Scientists on Earth are studying planets like this to find out if they could support life. Isn't that exciting?"

Alex nodded, imagining friendly alien creatures waving at them from afar. After exploring the orange plains of Gliese 667 Cc, they hopped back into the spaceship and set off to their next destination, Kepler-22b.

Kepler-22b was a world covered in vast oceans and dotted with small islands. "This planet is bigger than Earth and has more water. Imagine the kind of sea creatures that could live here!" Luna said as they floated above the turquoise waters.

"Maybe there are giant fish or talking dolphins!" Alex giggled, peering down at the sparkling sea below.

"Anything is possible in the universe, Alex," Luna replied with a wink.

Their adventure continued to TRAPPIST-1e, a planet that fascinated scientists because it was also in the habitable zone of its star, just like Earth. As they strolled along the violet sands, Luna explained how this planet might have the right conditions for life to thrive.

"Every exoplanet we visit teaches us something new about the universe and the possibility of life beyond Earth," Luna said, looking at the sky, which was filled with more stars and planets than Alex could count.

Feeling a bit tired from their interstellar travels, Alex and Luna decided it was time to head back home. As the spaceship journeyed back to Earth, Alex thought about all the amazing exoplanets they had visited.

"Thank you, Luna, for showing me how vast and wonderful the universe is. I'll never look at the night sky the same way again," Alex said, grateful for the incredible adventure.

"You're welcome, Alex. Remember, the universe is full of mysteries waiting to be discovered. Keep looking up at the stars and wondering. Who knows? Maybe one day, you'll find the answers to those mysteries," Luna said, as they landed softly in Alex's backyard.

With a final wave, Luna boarded the spaceship and zoomed off into the night, leaving Alex gazing up at the stars, dreaming about future adventures among the exoplanets.

And so, Alex learned that the universe was much bigger than they had ever imagined, filled with endless possibilities and wonders. From that day on, Alex never stopped dreaming about the exoplanets and the secrets they held, hopeful that one day, humanity would discover life beyond Earth.

The End.

THE MULTICULTURAL MUSIC FESTIVAL

Once upon a time, in a vibrant town filled with colors and joy, a special event was about to take place. It was no ordinary event, for it was the "Multicultural Music Festival," a day when music from all corners of the world would come together in harmony. The whole town buzzed with excitement, and everyone, from the tiniest toddler to the eldest elder, looked forward to it.

In the heart of this town, there lived a young girl named Mia and her best friend, a cheerful boy named Leo. Mia and Leo were inseparable, and they shared a deep love for music. They had been waiting for the festival all year long, dreaming about the wonderful instruments and the beautiful songs they would hear.

The morning of the festival dawned bright and clear. Mia and Leo, holding hands, raced through the streets, following the melody that floated on the breeze. As they arrived at the festival grounds, their eyes widened in wonder. There were flags fluttering in the wind, each representing a different country, and stages set up for performers.

Their first stop was at a stage where a group from Africa was performing. The air vibrated with the deep, rhythmic beats of the drums. Mia and Leo felt the music in their feet and couldn't help but dance along. They learned that the drums were called Djembes, and each rhythm told a different story.

Next, they wandered to a stage where a lady in a beautiful sari played the sitar, an instrument from India. The strings of the sitar weaved a magical spell, and its melody carried them to far-off lands of mystery and wonder. The lady smiled and explained how the sitar could express emotions, from joy to sadness, all through its music.

As the day went on, Mia and Leo explored more and more.

They listened to the enchanting sounds of the Scottish bagpipes, marveling at how the music sounded like the wind over the hills. They were captivated by the soothing melodies of the Japanese koto, its notes as delicate as the cherry blossoms in spring.

At each stage, they met new friends from different countries, each sharing their own unique music and stories. They danced with children from Brazil to the lively beats of the Samba, and they clapped along with the flamboyant rhythms of Spanish flamenco dancers.

As the sun began to set, the festival organizers announced the grand finale. All the musicians from the day gathered on the main stage, bringing their instruments with them. Mia and Leo watched in awe as the performers prepared to play together.

And then, the music began. It was unlike anything Mia and Leo had ever heard. The drums, the sitar, the bagpipes, the koto, and all the other instruments from around the world played in unison. It was a symphony of cultures, a celebration of diversity, all coming together in harmony. The music rose and fell, telling stories of distant lands, of joy and sorrow, of peace and love.

Mia and Leo, along with everyone else at the festival, were mesmerized. They realized that even though they came from different places and spoke different languages, music was a language they all understood. It brought them together, uniting them in a way words never could.

As the final note echoed through the night, the crowd erupted into applause. Mia and Leo, hand in hand, smiled at each other, their hearts full of joy and their minds filled with the beautiful melodies they had heard.

They knew that the Multicultural Music Festival was more than just an event; it was a reminder of the beauty in diversity and the power of music to connect us all. And as they walked home under the starlit sky, they hummed the melody of the world, a melody that would stay with them forever.

The End.

THE SAMURAI'S HONOR

In a land far away, nestled between rolling hills and whispering forests, was a place called Feudal Japan. This was a land of wonder, where the cherry blossoms painted the sky pink in spring and the air carried tales of bravery and honor.

In a small village surrounded by vast rice fields, lived a young samurai named Hiro. Hiro was not just any samurai; he was kind, brave, and most importantly, he held the code of honor close to his heart. This code, known as *Bushido*, taught him to be respectful, courageous, and loyal.

One sunny morning, as the village was just waking up, Hiro received a message from the Emperor. The Emperor's precious cherry blossom tree, which brought peace and joy to the land, had mysteriously stopped blooming. Without its blossoms, the people felt a shadow of sadness over the kingdom. Hiro knew it was his duty to help, so he bowed deeply and set off on his journey, his samurai sword by his side.

As Hiro traveled through forests and over mountains, he met many friends along the way. First, he encountered a wise old crane by a crystal-clear lake. The crane bowed gracefully and shared a secret, "True strength lies not in your sword, Hiro, but in the purity of your heart."

Next, Hiro met a playful fox in the forest, with fur as red as the setting sun. The fox giggled and said, "Remember, Hiro, cleverness and wit can overcome any obstacle."

Finally, as Hiro climbed the tallest mountain, he met a powerful dragon. The dragon roared mightily but spoke with kindness, "Honor and bravery will guide you, young samurai. Trust in them, and you will find what you seek."

With these words echoing in his heart, Hiro finally reached the Emperor's garden. But what he saw puzzled him. The cherry blossom tree stood tall, yet not a single petal bloomed. Hiro sat down and meditated, thinking deeply about the words of his new friends.

Then, it dawned on him. The tree needed not just water and sunlight, but love and respect to bloom. Hiro bowed to the tree, speaking words of gratitude and admiration for its beauty and the joy it brought to the people. As he did, a soft wind began to blow, and one by one, pink blossoms started to bloom, filling the garden with a sweet fragrance and the air with laughter and happiness.

The Emperor arrived, astonished by the miracle. Hiro explained, "Your Majesty, it was not my sword that brought the blossoms back, but honoring the spirit of the tree and the land."

The Emperor smiled, his heart filled with joy. "Hiro, you have shown true samurai spirit. You understood that honor, respect, and love are the greatest powers of all."
Hiro bowed, feeling the warmth of his journey's lessons. As he returned to his village, the cherry blossoms seemed to dance in the wind, celebrating his return.

From that day on, Hiro shared his adventure with everyone, teaching them about the *Bushido* code and how to live a life of honor, respect, and courage. The people listened, their hearts open, and the land of Feudal Japan flourished like never before, a testament to the true power of the samurai's honor.

And so, in the glow of the setting sun, among the blooming cherry blossoms, the tale of Hiro, the young samurai, became a cherished story, passed down through generations, reminding all of the beauty and strength found in kindness, wisdom, and the honor of the samurai.

The End.

THE MONARCH BUTTERFLY MIGRATION

Once upon a time, in a lush green meadow filled with colorful flowers and bustling with life, there lived a young monarch butterfly named Mariposa.

Mariposa was not like any other butterfly; she was about to embark on a grand adventure that many had taken before her, but each time, it felt as unique as the first. This journey was the great migration, a journey that monarch butterflies have embarked on for generations, traveling thousands of miles to find a warmer home for the winter.

Mariposa fluttered her delicate wings in excitement, the orange and black patterns shimmering in the sunlight. She had heard stories from her elders about the vast distances they covered, the places they visited, and the challenges they faced along the way. But Mariposa was not afraid; she was eager to see the world beyond her meadow and learn the secrets of the great migration.

Before her journey began, Mariposa's mother gathered her and her siblings to share the wisdom of the monarchs. "The migration is not just a journey," she said, "it's a dance with the wind, a testament to our resilience, and a reminder of the importance of caring for the places we call home, even if it's just for a season."

With her mother's words in her heart, Mariposa set off into the sky, joining a flutter of monarchs, each one a vibrant splash against the blue canvas above. As they flew, Mariposa learned the first lesson of migration: teamwork. Together, the monarchs created a living river of orange and black, each butterfly's wings helping to lift the others, making the long journey easier for all.

Their path led them over fields and forests, rivers and cities, each landscape a new world to discover. Mariposa was amazed by the beauty of the earth below, but she also saw the challenges. There were places where trees had been cut down, leaving less space for the butterflies to rest, and skies filled with smoke that made it hard to breathe.

As they traveled, Mariposa and her friends stopped to rest in gardens and meadows that were friendly to butterflies, places where humans had planted milkweed and other flowers that monarchs need to thrive. Mariposa realized the second lesson of migration: the importance of conservation. She saw that when people and nature worked together, life flourished.

The journey was long, and there were days when the wind blew cold and the rain made it hard to fly. But Mariposa remembered her mother's words and found strength in the flutter of wings around her. Finally, after many days and nights, Mariposa and her companions reached their winter home, a forest filled with trees that seemed to touch the sky, their branches heavy with the weight of thousands of monarchs.

There, in the warmth of the forest, Mariposa discovered the final lesson of the migration: the miracle of life's cycles. She learned that the great migration was not just about finding warmer weather, but about completing a cycle that had been going on for generations, a cycle that connected Mariposa to her past and to her future.

As spring returned, Mariposa knew it was time to make the journey back to the meadow where she was born. She felt a deep connection to the earth and a commitment to protect the beauty of the world for future generations of monarchs.

Mariposa's journey was more than just a migration; it was a lesson in courage, teamwork, and the importance of caring for our planet. She returned to her meadow not just as a butterfly, but as a guardian of the earth, ready to share her story and inspire others to take part in the great dance of life.

And so, as Mariposa fluttered among the flowers of her home, her wings seemed to carry the whispers of a thousand journeys, a reminder of the delicate balance of nature and the role each of us plays in preserving it for the generations to come.

The End.

THE CRYSTAL CAVES'
HIDDEN MAGIC

Once upon a time, in a land filled with rolling hills and endless skies, there was a small, cozy village. The children of this village were always curious, their eyes sparkling with wonder for the world around them. Among these children, Mia and Alex stood out for their adventurous spirits. One sunny morning, they stumbled upon an old, wise villager, Mr. Jasper, who told them tales of the Crystal Caves hidden deep beneath the earth, a place where magic danced in the air, and the stones told stories of the ancient world.

Excited by Mr. Jasper's stories, Mia and Alex decided they must see these caves for themselves. They packed their little backpacks with essentials – a flashlight, a map, a compass, and a small notebook to jot down their discoveries. As they waved goodbye to their village, their hearts beat with anticipation for the adventure that lay ahead.

Their journey took them through the whispering forests and over babbling brooks until they arrived at the entrance of the Crystal Caves. The entrance was hidden away behind a curtain of ivy, just as Mr. Jasper had described. With a deep breath and a shared look of excitement, they pushed aside the ivy and stepped into the cool, dimly lit cave.

As their eyes adjusted to the dim light, they were struck by the beauty before them. The walls of the cave glittered with thousands of crystals, each one casting its own rainbow as the light from Mia and Alex's flashlights danced across them. The children were in awe. "It's like a treasure chest of jewels!" Mia exclaimed, her voice echoing softly through the cavern.

Alex opened the notebook and began to sketch the crystals, while Mia used her flashlight to explore further. She discovered that each crystal formation was unique. Some were tall and pointed like the towers of a castle, while others spread across the ceiling like a blanket of stars.

As they ventured deeper into the caves, they found a large, open chamber. In the center of the chamber stood a magnificent crystal unlike any they had seen before. It was as tall as a tree, and its colors shifted and changed with every step they took. Mr. Jasper had called this the Heart of the Cave, a special crystal that held the magic of the earth.

Mia and Alex approached the Heart of the Cave, and as they did, the crystal began to glow softly. It was as if the crystal was alive, sensing their presence. They reached out to touch it, and as their fingers brushed against its surface, a warm, gentle light enveloped them. In that moment, they felt a deep connection to the earth and all its wonders.

The Heart of the Cave whispered to them, not in words, but in feelings and images. It showed them how the crystals formed over millions of years, from drops of water and minerals seeping through the earth, layer by layer, growing into the magnificent formations they saw today. It taught them about the patience of nature and the beauty that comes from taking time to grow.

Feeling grateful for this gift of knowledge, Mia and Alex placed their hands on their hearts, promising to always respect and protect the wonders of the natural world. As they made their promise, the Heart of the Cave glowed even brighter for a moment, then returned to its gentle shimmer.

With hearts full of joy and minds brimming with new knowledge, Mia and Alex knew it was time to return to their village. They made their way back through the Crystal Caves, pausing to admire the beauty around them one last time. As they emerged into the sunlight, they felt as if they were leaving a part of themselves behind in the caves, a testament to their journey and the magic they had discovered.

Back in the village, they shared their adventure with Mr. Jasper and the other villagers, telling them about the Heart of the Cave and the lessons it had taught them. The villagers listened in wonder, and from that day forward, they looked at the world around them with a new sense of appreciation and awe.

Mia and Alex's adventure in the Crystal Caves became a cherished story in the village, a reminder of the magic hidden just beneath our feet and the importance of protecting the natural beauty of our world. And so, the Crystal Caves' hidden magic lived on, not just in the earth, but in the hearts of all who heard the tale.

The End.

ANCIENT GREEK
ODYSSEY

Once upon a time, in a land not so far away, there was a curious young
child named Emma. Emma loved stories and adventures, and she always

wanted to learn something new. One sunny morning, while flipping through the pages of a big book, Emma stumbled upon a picture of a majestic temple with a caption that read, "Ancient Greece."

Her eyes sparkled with curiosity as she wondered what ancient Greece was all about. Emma decided she wanted to go on an adventure to this magical place and learn all there was to know. And so, her journey to Ancient Greece began.

With a little bit of magic and a lot of imagination, Emma found herself in Ancient Greece. She stood in front of a beautiful temple dedicated to the goddess Athena. Emma was amazed by its grandeur and wondered who Athena was. Nearby, she saw an old man sitting under a shady olive tree.

Emma approached the old man and asked, "Excuse me, sir, could you tell me about this temple and the goddess Athena?"

The old man smiled and began to tell her stories about Athena, the goddess of wisdom and courage. He explained that people in Ancient Greece believed in many gods and goddesses, and they often built magnificent temples like this one to honor them. Emma listened intently, absorbing the knowledge like a sponge.

As Emma continued her journey, she encountered a wise philosopher named Socrates. He was sitting on a stone, surrounded by young students eager to learn. Emma joined them and listened as Socrates asked thought-provoking questions and encouraged everyone to think deeply.

Socrates said, "The unexamined life is not worth living," and Emma realized that it meant it was essential to ask questions and understand the world around her. She thanked Socrates for the valuable lesson and continued on her adventure.

Next, Emma visited the city of Athens, the birthplace of democracy. She watched as people gathered in a grand assembly to make important decisions together. The idea of everyone having a say in their government fascinated Emma. She learned that Ancient Greeks believed in the power of the people.

Emma also visited the famous Olympic Games, where she watched athletes from all over Greece compete in various sports. She marveled at their strength and skill and learned that the Olympic Games were held to honor the god Zeus.

One sunny afternoon, Emma sat by the shore and listened to the mesmerizing tales of ancient Greek mythology. A storyteller named Apollo told her stories of brave heroes like Hercules, wise gods like Zeus, and enchanting creatures like the beautiful sirens. Emma's imagination soared as she heard these incredible stories.

One night, as Emma lay under the twinkling stars, she thought about all the amazing things she had learned on her journey through Ancient Greece. She realized that knowledge was a treasure, and her adventure had been like a magical odyssey.

But it was time for Emma to return home. She closed her eyes and made a wish. With a sprinkle of stardust, she found herself back in her room, surrounded by her favorite books. Emma knew that her journey to Ancient Greece had been a special gift, and she felt grateful for all the knowledge she had gained.

From that day on, Emma continued to ask questions, explore the world around her, and share the stories of Ancient Greece with her friends. She knew that the spirit of adventure and the love of learning would stay with her forever.

And so, Emma's Ancient Greek Odyssey became a cherished memory, inspiring her and many others to embrace the wonders of the world and the magic of knowledge. And they all lived happily ever after, in a world filled with endless curiosity and imagination.

The End.

THE WORLDWIDE
FAMILY REUNION

Once upon a time, in a colorful world filled with endless possibilities, there was a magical event known as "The Worldwide Family Reunion." This incredible celebration brought together families from all corners of the world, celebrating the unique cultures and the beautiful bonds that connected them.

The reunion was held in a vast, enchanting park, where the grass was as green as emeralds, and the sky was a brilliant shade of blue. Families from every continent received special invitations that fluttered like butterflies and shimmered like rainbows. It was a day everyone had been eagerly waiting for, a day to meet cousins, uncles, aunts, and grandparents they had never even known existed.

In a little village nestled among rolling hills, a young girl named Mia was getting ready for the big day. She carefully chose a traditional dress adorned with vibrant colors and patterns, reflecting her family's heritage. Mia's heart danced with excitement as she thought about meeting family members from different parts of the world.

As the sun began to rise, Mia and her family set off on a grand adventure. They traveled through dense forests, crossed sparkling rivers, and climbed tall mountains to reach the magical park. Along the way, they met friendly animals and heard enchanting stories from the people they encountered, each one teaching them something new about the world.

When they finally arrived at the park, Mia was greeted by a breathtaking sight. There were tents and pavilions representing every culture imaginable, with flags fluttering in the breeze and the delicious aroma of diverse cuisines filling the air. People were singing songs, dancing to unique rhythms, and sharing stories about their families and traditions.

Mia's eyes widened with wonder as she explored the different corners of the park. She tasted delicious sushi from Japan, danced to the lively beats of drums from Africa, and listened to enchanting tales from her distant relatives in India. Mia's heart swelled with pride as she learned about her own family's customs and shared them with others, like making paper lanterns for Chinese New Year and preparing traditional Italian pasta.

Throughout the day, Mia made new friends from around the world, and together, they created a masterpiece of unity and friendship. They painted a gigantic mural that depicted their diverse cultures, each contributing their unique touch to the masterpiece. Mia added a bright sun to the painting, symbolizing hope, love, and the warmth that comes from connecting with others.

As the sun began to set, a hush fell over the park, and everyone gathered in a vast, grassy field. The sky was adorned with stars, and the moon cast a gentle glow on the happy faces of families from every corner of the Earth. Mia's heart was filled with joy and gratitude for this magical day.

A wise elder from a far-off land stepped forward and spoke to the crowd. "Today," he said, "we have learned that we are all part of a beautiful tapestry, woven together by the threads of love, culture, and family. Though our traditions and languages may be different, our hearts beat as one. We are all part of the same worldwide family."

With those words, the sky erupted in a burst of brilliant fireworks, painting the night with colors from every culture. The crowd cheered and clapped, and Mia felt the warm embrace of her newfound family. It was a celebration of unity and diversity, a day that would be remembered forever.

As Mia and her family left the park, they carried with them the memories of The Worldwide Family Reunion, the laughter, the love, and the knowledge that no matter where they came from, they were all connected in a global family filled with endless possibilities.

And so, dear children, always remember that the world is a vast and colorful place, filled with people who may seem different on the outside but share the same love, hopes, and dreams on the inside. Just like Mia, you too can be a part of the worldwide family, celebrating the beautiful diversity that makes our world so extraordinary.

The End.

VOYAGE TO VENUS

Once upon a time, in a colorful and magical world, there lived a group of curious and adventurous friends. Their names were Sammy the brave squirrel, Lila the clever rabbit, and Timmy the imaginative turtle. They were the best of friends and loved going on exciting adventures together.

One sunny morning, as they sat near their favorite pond, Sammy had a brilliant idea. "I heard there's a mysterious planet called Venus up in the sky. Why don't we go on a journey to Venus?" he asked, his eyes sparkling with excitement.

Lila, the clever rabbit, was intrigued. "That sounds like an amazing adventure, Sammy! But how do we get there?"
Timmy, the imaginative turtle, put on his thinking cap. "I've been reading about space travel in my books. We'll need a spaceship and some help from our scientist friend, Professor Owl."

The friends hopped, scurried, and swam to Professor Owl's treehouse, where he was busy with his experiments. "Professor Owl," Sammy said, "we want to go on a journey to Venus! Can you help us build a spaceship?"

The wise old owl looked at the eager friends and smiled. "Of course, my young adventurers! I will help you build a spaceship, but you must promise to be careful and learn all you can about the challenges of space travel."

The friends nodded enthusiastically and got to work with Professor Owl. They gathered all the materials they needed, including shiny metal, bolts, and buttons. They worked tirelessly, day and night, until their spaceship was ready to launch.

Finally, the day of the big adventure arrived. The friends stood in front of their spaceship, which they had named "Starry Voyager." Professor Owl gave them some important instructions. "Remember, space is very different from our world. It's extremely cold, there's no air to breathe, and you'll float in zero gravity. You must wear your space suits at all times and stay inside the spaceship."

With their helmets on and their hearts full of excitement, Sammy, Lila, and Timmy climbed into Starry Voyager. They counted down from ten, and then, with a whoosh, they were off! The spaceship soared into the sky, leaving behind their magical world.

As they journeyed through space, they marveled at the twinkling stars and the beauty of the universe. "Look, there's the moon!" exclaimed Timmy, pointing at the familiar sight.

But as they approached Venus, they faced their first challenge. The spaceship began to shake, and alarms rang loudly. "What's happening?" cried Lila.

Professor Owl's voice came through the speaker, "Don't worry, my friends. We're entering Venus's thick atmosphere. Hold on tight!"

With a bumpy ride, Starry Voyager entered the cloudy atmosphere of Venus. The planet was shrouded in thick clouds, making it hard to see. "It's so different from our world," said Sammy, gazing out of the window.

Finally, they landed on the surface of Venus. As they stepped out of the spaceship in their space suits, they felt the extreme heat and saw the rocky terrain. "Venus is the hottest planet in our solar system," explained Timmy. "It's like a giant oven!"

They explored Venus carefully, taking notes and collecting samples. They discovered that the planet had many volcanoes and strange rocks. It was a challenging but exciting adventure.

After a few hours, they returned to Starry Voyager and prepared for their journey back home. As they left Venus and headed back towards their magical world, they couldn't help but smile at the knowledge they had gained.

When they landed safely back in their world, they rushed to Professor Owl to share their incredible journey. "We did it! We traveled to Venus and learned so much about space!" they exclaimed.

Professor Owl beamed with pride. "You did a remarkable job, my young adventurers. You faced challenges with courage and curiosity, just as I hoped you would."

Sammy, Lila, and Timmy realized that while space travel was full of challenges, it was also full of wonder and knowledge. They were grateful for their friendship, their wise mentor, and the incredible journey they had embarked upon.

And so, their magical world continued to be filled with adventures and discoveries, as Sammy, Lila, and Timmy cherished their voyage to Venus and looked forward to many more adventures in the future.

The End.

EXPEDITION TO THE ARCTIC CIRCLE

Once upon a time, in a world filled with wonders and adventures, there was a curious little girl named Mia and her best friend, a playful polar bear cub named Paws. Mia lived in a colorful village near the Arctic Circle, where the snow sparkled like diamonds and the northern lights danced in the sky.

One sunny morning, Mia and Paws decided to go on an exciting expedition to explore the Arctic. They put on their warmest coats, packed a backpack with snacks and a map, and set off on their adventure.
As they journeyed across the snowy landscape, Mia and Paws marveled at the icy mountains that touched the sky. They slid down snowy hills, giggling and laughing, and made snow angels in the fluffy snow.

Soon, they came across a group of Inuit people, the indigenous people of the Arctic. The Inuit welcomed Mia and Paws with open arms and shared their fascinating stories and traditions. They taught Mia how to fish through a hole in the ice and showed her how to build an igloo.

Mia was amazed to learn that the Inuit had lived in the Arctic for thousands of years, adapting to the cold climate and respecting the land and animals. She realized how important it was to understand and appreciate different cultures.

Next, Mia and Paws met a scientist named Dr. Snowflake, who was studying the Arctic climate. Dr. Snowflake explained to Mia how the Arctic was changing due to global warming. She showed Mia and Paws how the ice was melting and how it affected the polar bears and other animals.

Mia felt sad to see the changes in the Arctic but was inspired by Dr. Snowflake's passion for helping the environment. She learned that even small actions, like recycling and saving energy, could make a big difference.

As the sun began to set, painting the sky with hues of pink and orange, Mia and Paws knew it was time to head back home. They thanked the Inuit people and Dr. Snowflake for the wonderful experiences and lessons.

On their way back, Mia and Paws saw a family of polar bears playing near the shore. Paws joined them, and Mia watched with joy as they played together. She realized how special the Arctic was and how important it was to protect it for future generations.

As the first stars appeared in the night sky, Mia and Paws reached their village, their hearts full of memories and new knowledge. They promised each other to always remember their amazing expedition and the importance of caring for our planet.

Mia shared her adventure with her family and friends, inspiring them with stories of the Arctic's beauty and the need to protect it. She knew that even though she was just a little girl, she could make a big difference in the world.

And so, Mia and Paws continued to explore and learn, knowing that every adventure brought new lessons and a chance to make the world a better place.

The End.

THE DESERT'S SECRET LIFE

Once upon a time, in a vast and sun-drenched desert, where the sands shimmered like gold under the sky's azure embrace, there was a secret world unknown to many. This desert, though it looked empty and quiet, was bustling with life – a magical place where every creature and plant had a special story to tell.

One bright morning, a curious little lizard named Leo awoke from his slumber beneath a warm rock. Leo was no ordinary lizard; he had the most vibrant, patterned skin, which helped him blend in with the colorful sands and stones of the desert. This was his first adaptation, a gift from the desert to protect him.

Leo decided to embark on a journey to discover more secrets of the desert. As he scurried across the sand, he met Ellie, an eagle soaring high above. Ellie had keen eyesight, able to spot the tiniest of creatures from up in the sky. She shared with Leo how she could glide effortlessly for hours, searching for food, thanks to her wide wings – another marvel of the desert life.

Together, they flew and walked, exploring the rolling dunes. They stumbled upon a patch of cacti, standing tall and proud. Among them was Catherine, a cheerful cactus with bright pink flowers. Catherine was unique; she could store water in her thick, fleshy stems for months, a perfect adaptation for surviving in a place where rain was a rare guest.

As the day wore on, they met Omar, the owl, who had just woken up in his burrow. Omar had big, round eyes that helped him see in the dark. He explained how he hunted at night when the desert was cooler, and how his soft feathers allowed him to fly silently to surprise his prey.

Not far from Omar's burrow, they encountered Sandy, the clever desert fox. Sandy had large ears that not only helped her hear tiny insects under the sand but also kept her cool in the scorching heat. She showed them her den, dug deep into the sand, where she stayed during the hottest part of the day. The sun began to set, painting the sky in shades of orange, pink, and purple. It was a signal for nocturnal creatures to emerge. Leo and his new friends watched in awe as the desert transformed. Night-blooming flowers opened, releasing sweet fragrances, and nocturnal insects buzzed in the cool air.

They met a friendly tarantula named Toby, who danced across the sand. Toby explained how his hairy legs helped him sense vibrations on the ground, so he could quickly find food or escape predators. Even in the darkness, the desert was alive and thriving!

As the moon climbed higher in the night sky, a gentle breeze whispered secrets of the desert. It told tales of ancient rivers that once flowed through the land, of mountains that watched over the sands for centuries, and of stars that guided travelers on their journeys.

Leo realized that the desert, with its harsh sun and scarce water, was not just a place of survival but of wonder and magic. Every creature, every plant had adapted in their own special way, not just to live, but to thrive in this beautiful, mysterious world.

The night grew deeper, and it was time for Leo to return to his warm rock. He bid goodbye to his new friends, promising to explore more secrets another day.

As Leo nestled under his rock, he smiled, thinking of all the incredible adaptations and friendships he had discovered. The desert, he realized, was not empty or lifeless at all. It was a vibrant ecosystem, full of hidden stories and secret lives, just waiting to be explored.

And so, under the twinkling stars, the desert whispered its lullabies, rocking Leo to sleep, assuring him that tomorrow would be another day of adventure in the secret life of the desert.

And they all lived happily ever after, in their unique, adapted, and magical desert home.

The End.

THE GNOME'S GARDEN OF WONDERS

Once upon a time, in a lush, green forest filled with whispers of wildlife and the scent of fresh earth, there lived a cheerful gnome named Gilbert.

Gilbert was no ordinary gnome; he was the guardian of a magical garden, a place where wonders bloomed and secrets were nestled in every leaf and petal.

One sunny morning, a group of curious children wandered into the forest, their eyes wide with wonder. They had heard tales of Gilbert's Garden of Wonders, a place where plants could sing and butterflies glowed like little lanterns.

"Hello, little adventurers!" Gilbert greeted them with a warm smile, his red hat twinkling in the sunlight. "Welcome to my garden, a place where magic grows and every flower has a story to tell."

The children followed Gilbert on a winding path through the garden. The first stop was a bed of giggling daisies. "These are the Giggling Daisies," Gilbert explained. "They laugh to spread joy and remind us to find happiness in the little things."

Next, they came upon a pond where frogs with shimmering, rainbow-colored skin leaped joyfully from lily pad to lily pad. "These are the Rainbow Frogs," Gilbert said. "They teach us that beauty comes in many colors and forms."

As they walked, the children saw trees with leaves that changed colors with the children's emotions, and a patch of shy sunflowers that would only bloom when sung to. Gilbert taught the children songs of nature, their voices mingling with the rustling leaves and chirping birds.

Then, they reached the heart of the garden, where a magnificent tree stood. Its branches were laden with fruits of all kinds, some the children recognized, and some they had never seen before. "This is the Tree of Togetherness," Gilbert explained. "It bears fruits from all over the world, reminding us that though we may be different, we all share the same roots."

Near the tree, a group of tiny, glittering creatures fluttered around. "Meet the Whispering Pixies," said Gilbert with a grin. "They carry the secrets of the garden. If you listen closely, they might share a secret or two with you."

As the day turned into evening, Gilbert led the children to a clearing where fireflies danced in the twilight. "The garden is not just about plants and creatures," he said, sitting down on a patch of soft moss. "It's about the magic within us — the curiosity, joy, and wonder that makes the world a beautiful place."

The children, tired but happy, lay on the grass, looking up at the stars peeking through the treetops. Gilbert strummed a small guitar, and the garden seemed to hum along, lulling them into a peaceful rest.

In their dreams, the children roamed the garden, each finding their own wonder: a flower that whispered sweet dreams, a butterfly that painted rainbows in the sky, and a friendly tree that told ancient tales.

When they awoke, the first light of dawn was painting the sky in shades of pink and orange. Gilbert was still there, smiling kindly. "The garden is always here for you," he said. "Remember, every plant, every creature, has a story, just like each one of you. Carry the magic of this place in your hearts, and share its wonders with the world."
As the children left the garden, they looked back to see Gilbert waving, his garden glowing softly in the morning light. They knew they would return, for the Garden of Wonders was not just a place, but a feeling — a reminder of the magic and beauty in the world and within themselves.

And so, the Gnome's Garden of Wonders lived on, not just in the heart of the forest, but in the hearts of all who visited, spreading joy, wonder, and the magic of nature to everyone, everywhere.

The End.

THE BIG FAMILY
COOKING CONTEST

Once upon a time, in a cozy little town surrounded by rolling hills and
sparkling streams, there was a buzz of excitement in the air. The reason for

all the excitement was the upcoming event that had everyone talking - The Big Family Cooking Contest!

In this special town, families came from all corners of the globe, each bringing with them their unique traditions and, most importantly, their delicious recipes. The Mayor of the town, Mrs. Butterbean, had a brilliant idea to celebrate this diversity. She announced, "Let's have a cooking contest where each family will prepare a dish from their homeland. It will be a feast of flavors from around the world!"

The news spread like wildfire, and soon, every household was bustling with preparations. There were pots and pans clanging, spoons and whisks twirling, and a symphony of scents filled the air.

The Johnsons, known for their love of adventure, decided to make a spicy curry from India, with a secret ingredient passed down through generations. Little Timmy Johnson was in charge of adding the spices, making sure each spoonful was measured with care.

Next door, the O'Reilly family, with roots in Italy, chose to make a hearty lasagna layered with homemade pasta, rich tomato sauce, and gooey cheese. Mia O'Reilly, just five years old, wore her chef's hat and helped by carefully placing the basil leaves on top, giving it her special touch.
Across the street, the Chen family was busy preparing a traditional Chinese dumpling recipe. The children, Lin and Ming, were experts at folding the dumplings into perfect little crescents, their small fingers working with surprising skill.

And then there were the Garcias, who brought the vibrant flavors of Mexico to the table with their colorful enchiladas, each one wrapped with love and sprinkled with laughter by the youngest Garcia, Sofia.

As the big day arrived, the entire town gathered in the main square, which had been transformed into a gigantic outdoor kitchen. There were cooking stations decorated with flags from around the world, and the air was alive with the sounds of sizzling, chopping, and the cheerful chatter of families working together.

Mayor Butterbean, wearing her apron and chef's hat, declared the contest open. "Ready, set, cook!" she exclaimed, and the square erupted into a whirlwind of culinary activity.

As the sun dipped below the hills, painting the sky in shades of orange and pink, the cooking came to an end. Each family presented their dish on a long table that stretched across the square, turning it into a rainbow of cuisines.

The tasting began, with everyone in town moving from one dish to the next, their taste buds taking them on a journey across the globe. The children, with their faces painted with sauces and spices, giggled as they tried new flavors, some making funny faces at the unfamiliar tastes but always eager for the next bite.

After much deliberation, Mayor Butterbean announced that the contest was too close to call. "Each dish tells a story of heritage and home, and together, they weave a tapestry of our town's shared history and friendship. Today, we are all winners!"

The square erupted in cheers and applause, as everyone agreed that the true prize was the joy of coming together, sharing, and celebrating the diverse threads that bound them into one big, happy family.

As the stars twinkled above, the night ended with music and dancing, the air filled with the harmony of different languages and laughter, a perfect ending to a day that celebrated the beauty of diversity through the universal language of food.

And so, The Big Family Cooking Contest became an annual tradition, eagerly awaited by all, not just for the competition but for the chance to come together, to share and to learn from one another, creating memories that would be savored just like the delectable dishes that brought them all together.

From that day on, the children of the town grew up knowing that no matter where you come from, the kitchen is a place where love is the most important ingredient, and a meal is so much more than just food on a plate. It's a story, a memory, a piece of home. And in their cozy little town, every dish had a place at the table, just like every person had a place in their big, loving family.

And they all lived deliciously ever after.

The End.

THE MYSTERY OF THE MISSING MOONS

Once upon a time, in the far reaches of the Milky Way, there was a beautiful planet named Celestia, known far and wide for its seven sparkling moons.

Each moon shone with a unique color and had its own special magic. The people of Celestia loved to gaze up at their shimmering moons every night, feeling safe and cherished under their gentle glow.

But one morning, something very strange happened. The people of Celestia woke up to find that one of their beloved moons had disappeared! There was a buzz of worry among the villagers as they looked up at the sky, seeing only six moons where there should have been seven.

The king of Celestia called upon the wisest and bravest explorer of the land, young Captain Luna and her trusty space dog, Comet, to solve the mystery of the missing moon. Captain Luna was known for her curiosity and courage, and she had a special spaceship that could zoom through the stars.

Before setting off on their adventure, Captain Luna and Comet visited the grand library of Celestia to learn more about their moons and the solar system. The wise old librarian, Mr. Starlight, showed them ancient books filled with cosmic tales and star maps. They learned about the planets, stars, and the vast universe beyond their own world.

Armed with knowledge and courage, Captain Luna and Comet blasted off into the starry sky in their spaceship, leaving a trail of stardust behind. Their first stop was the Moon of Emerald, where they hoped to find clues about the disappearance.

On the Emerald Moon, they met a friendly moon creature named Glowy, who glimmered with a soft green light. Glowy hadn't seen the missing moon but mentioned that lately, the space winds had been acting very strangely, swirling around the moons in unusual patterns.

Thanking Glowy, Captain Luna and Comet set off again, visiting each moon and meeting more moon creatures. They learned about gravity, the way planets and moons orbit, and how everything in the solar system is connected in a delicate dance.

Finally, on the Violet Moon, they met a wise old moon owl named Whisper, who had a twinkle in her eye. Whisper explained that the moons hadn't really disappeared; they were just hidden by a rare cosmic cloud, a fluffy, space cloud that sometimes drifted through their part of the galaxy, camouflaging anything it enveloped with its thick, misty folds.

"But don't worry," Whisper hooted softly, "The cosmic cloud is just passing by. Soon it will move on, and your missing moon will shine brightly once again."

Relieved but still curious, Captain Luna asked, "But why did the cosmic cloud come here?"

Whisper explained, "The universe is always changing, my dear. Cosmic clouds, comets, and even planets move in ways that sometimes bring them close to each other. It's all part of the great cosmic dance."

Thanking Whisper for her wisdom, Captain Luna and Comet hurried back to Celestia to share the good news. The people of Celestia were overjoyed to hear that their moon would soon return.

In the following nights, the people watched as the cosmic cloud slowly drifted away, revealing the missing moon, which shone brighter than ever. There was a grand celebration on Celestia, with music, dancing, and stories shared under the light of their complete family of moons.

Captain Luna and Comet became heroes, celebrated for their bravery and curiosity. They had taught everyone on Celestia the importance of scientific inquiry, patience, and the wonders of the cosmos.

And so, the mystery of the missing moons was solved, not by magic, but by the quest for knowledge and the courage to explore the unknown. The people of Celestia learned that the universe was full of mysteries waiting to be uncovered, and that sometimes, the answers were just beyond the stars, waiting for a curious mind to find them.

From then on, Captain Luna and Comet were always ready for their next adventure, knowing that each star in the sky and every planet in the solar system had its own story to tell. And the children of Celestia fell asleep each night under the watchful gaze of their seven moons, dreaming of their own space adventures among the stars.

And they all lived happily ever after, under the twinkling, ever-watchful eyes of the universe.

The End.

VOYAGE WITH THE VIKINGS

Once upon a time, in a land filled with majestic mountains and deep, mysterious fjords, lived a group of adventurous Vikings. Among them was a young Viking named Erik, known for his bright red hair and insatiable curiosity about the world beyond the shores of his homeland.

One sunny morning, Erik and his fellow Vikings prepared their sturdy longship, the Sea Dragon, for a grand voyage. The ship was a magnificent sight, with a beautifully carved dragon's head at the prow and a large, billowing sail that captured the wind's power.

As the Vikings set sail, Erik stood at the bow, feeling the fresh sea breeze on his face. The vast ocean stretched out before them, sparkling under the golden sun. Erik's heart swelled with excitement at the thought of exploring new lands and learning about distant cultures.

The Vikings were expert navigators, using the stars, the sun, and even the flight patterns of birds to guide their way across the open sea. Erik was fascinated by their skills and eagerly learned how to use a sun compass, a clever device that helped them determine their direction even when the sun was hidden by clouds.

As they ventured further from home, the Vikings encountered all sorts of wonders. They sailed through waters teeming with leaping fish and watched in awe as dolphins raced alongside the Sea Dragon, their sleek bodies gliding effortlessly through the waves.

One night, as Erik gazed up at the starry sky, an elder Viking named Olaf told him tales of the constellations. Erik learned about the Great Bear and the North Star, which were constant companions on their journey, always pointing the way north.

Days turned into weeks, and the Vikings explored many distant shores. They traded goods with people from other lands, exchanging furs and amber for spices and silk. Erik was amazed by the variety of languages and customs he encountered, and he collected small treasures from each place they visited to remember his adventures.
One of their most exciting discoveries was a lush, green island teeming with strange and exotic animals. Erik and the Vikings marveled at the colorful

birds and watched in wonder as herds of wild horses galloped across the rolling hills.

As they explored the island, they came across ancient ruins covered in mysterious runes. Erik was captivated by the intricate symbols, and the Vikings spent an entire day deciphering the messages carved into the stone. They learned about the island's history and the people who had lived there long ago, adding another piece to the puzzle of the world's vast and varied cultures.

But the voyage wasn't just about exploration and discovery. The Vikings also faced challenges, like fierce storms that tested their courage and skill. During one particularly wild tempest, Erik helped to steer the Sea Dragon through towering waves, working alongside his fellow Vikings to keep the ship safe and on course.

Throughout their journey, Erik and the Vikings celebrated their Norse culture, sharing stories of the gods and goddesses from their homeland. They sang traditional songs around the fire, their voices mingling with the crackle of flames and the distant roar of the sea.

As the voyage came to an end, and the Sea Dragon turned homeward, Erik felt a mix of sadness and excitement. He was eager to return to his family and friends, to share the tales of his adventures and the knowledge he had gained about the world.
When they finally arrived back in their village, the Vikings were greeted with cheers and open arms. Erik's eyes sparkled with the joy of homecoming, and his heart was full of the memories he had made on the high seas.

As he recounted his adventures, Erik realized that the greatest treasure he had brought back wasn't the exotic spices or the foreign trinkets, but the stories and experiences that had enriched his soul. He had learned about the importance of curiosity, courage, and camaraderie, values that would guide him for the rest of his life.

And so, under the glow of the northern lights, Erik's tale of the voyage with the Vikings came to a close, leaving all who listened dreaming of their own adventures in the wide, wonderful world.

The End.

THE WISE OLD OWL'S TALES

Once upon a time, in a lush green forest, there lived a wise old owl named Ollie. Ollie was known far and wide for his knowledge and kindness. Every evening, as the sun set and the stars began to twinkle, the animals of the forest would gather around Ollie's oak tree to listen to his tales.

One cool evening, as a gentle breeze rustled the leaves, Ollie welcomed his little friends. "Tonight," he hooted softly, "I will tell you about the nocturnal wonders of our forest."
The young animals shuffled closer, their eyes wide with curiosity.

"Our first tale," Ollie began, "is about Luna, the playful bat. While you all sleep, Luna dances in the moonlit sky. She uses her ears to see, listening to the echoes of her own calls to find her way and catch tiny insects for dinner. Luna teaches us to listen carefully to the world around us."

The animals gasped in amazement. They had never thought about how different the forest could be at night.
"Next," Ollie continued, "let me tell you about Felix, the clever fox. Felix has bright eyes and a sharp nose, helping him find food in the dark. He's quick and quiet, a master of hide-and-seek. From Felix, we learn to be observant and move gracefully through life."

The little animals giggled, imagining Felix playing hide-and-seek with them.

"Then there's Nora, the nightingale," Ollie went on. "She sings the most beautiful songs under the moon. Her melodies remind us that even in the quietest nights, there's beauty to be found if we listen."

The animals closed their eyes, picturing Nora's sweet songs filling the night air.

"Our last story for tonight is about Sammy, the sleepy hedgehog. When the sun sets, Sammy wakes up to explore. He may be small, but he's brave and always ready for an adventure. Sammy shows us that no matter our size, we can explore great things."

The animals nodded, feeling braver already.

As Ollie finished his stories, the animals felt a new appreciation for their forest friends and the wonders of the night. "Thank you, Ollie," they chirped, croaked, and whispered.

"You're welcome," Ollie hooted. "Remember, each creature in our forest, day or night, has a story and wisdom to share."

With hearts full of new tales and minds buzzing with lessons, the animals said goodnight to Ollie and scurried back to their homes, dreaming of nocturnal adventures.

And so, night after night, Ollie the wise old owl shared his tales, teaching the forest animals about the beauty and wisdom of their nighttime world.

The End.

THE HIDDEN TREASURES OF INDIA

Once upon a time, in the bustling city of Mumbai, there lived a curious and adventurous Indian boy named Arjun. Arjun loved stories about treasures and often dreamt of going on a treasure hunt. One sunny morning, while playing in his backyard, Arjun found a mysterious, old map hidden inside an ancient-looking trunk. The map was adorned with pictures of famous Indian landmarks, and in bold letters, it read, "The Hidden Treasures of India."

Filled with excitement, Arjun decided to embark on an adventure to discover these treasures. He waved goodbye to his parents and set out with the map in his hand. His first stop was the majestic Taj Mahal in Agra. As he marveled at the beautiful white marble monument, he noticed a shimmering piece of stone near a garden. It was a small, intricately carved marble elephant. Arjun carefully picked it up and realized it was the first hidden treasure!

Next, the map led Arjun to the vibrant city of Jaipur, known for its stunning palaces and forts. There, among the colorful markets, Arjun found a treasure hidden inside a clay pot - a traditional Rajasthani puppet dressed in bright clothes. Arjun was delighted and added it to his collection.

The adventure continued as Arjun traveled to the southern state of Kerala, famous for its lush greenery and backwaters. While enjoying a peaceful boat ride, he spotted something sparkling in the water. It was a beautiful necklace made of seashells and pearls, another hidden treasure!

Arjun's journey then took him to the snowy peaks of the Himalayas in the north. It was cold, and the mountains were challenging to climb, but Arjun was determined. At the top, he found a small Tibetan prayer flag, fluttering in the wind - his next treasure.

Feeling a bit tired but exhilarated, Arjun made his way to the east, to the ancient city of Varanasi. As he walked along the sacred Ganges River, he noticed a unique musical instrument abandoned on the steps. It was a sitar, exquisitely crafted and still in perfect tune. Arjun plucked the strings gently, and the music filled the air. This was his fifth treasure!

Finally, Arjun's map brought him back to Mumbai, where his adventure had begun. But there was one last treasure to find. As he wandered the streets of his hometown, he realized that the final treasure was not an object but the experiences and memories he had gathered. The friends he made, the stories he heard, and the beauty of India he witnessed were the real treasures.

Arjun returned home with his treasures and a heart full of joy. He shared his stories with his family, telling them about the beautiful places he visited and the wonderful people he met. His parents listened in awe and were proud of their brave son's journey.

That night, as Arjun went to bed, he looked at the treasures he had collected. He knew that these were just symbols of the rich culture, history, and diversity of India. The true treasure was the adventure itself and the knowledge that his country was a land of endless wonders. Arjun fell asleep with a smile, dreaming of his next adventure in the incredible land of India.

And so, Arjun learned that the greatest treasures are not always things you can hold in your hand but are often the experiences and memories that you keep in your heart.

The End.

THE FRIENDLY
VELOCIRAPTOR

Once upon a time, in a lush green forest filled with towering trees and sparkling streams, there lived a unique dinosaur named Vinnie. Vinnie was not like the other dinosaurs; he was a Velociraptor, but unlike the Velociraptors you might have heard about, Vinnie was incredibly friendly.

Vinnie loved to explore the forest, his bright eyes sparkling with curiosity. He had soft, feather-like scales that shimmered in the sunlight, and he walked gracefully on his two strong legs. Unlike what many stories said, Vinnie didn't roar menacingly; instead, he chirped cheerfully as he hopped around.

One sunny day, Vinnie met a group of young dinosaurs who were playing near a stream. They were startled at first, having heard scary stories about Velociraptors. But Vinnie greeted them with a gentle smile and a friendly wave of his claw.

"Hi there! I'm Vinnie the Velociraptor," he said in a sing-song voice. "I promise I'm not scary. I love making new friends!"

The young dinosaurs were amazed. They had never met a Velociraptor who was so friendly and kind. They introduced themselves one by one – Tara the Triceratops, Stevie the Stegosaurus, and Bronto the Brachiosaurus.

Vinnie was delighted to meet them and wanted to show them how much fun a Velociraptor could be. He invited them to join him on a little adventure through the forest, promising to share interesting facts about dinosaurs along the way.

As they walked, Vinnie told them about the different dinosaurs that lived in their forest. He explained that not all Velociraptors were scary and that they were actually quite smart and curious creatures. He showed them his sharp claws, not for hunting, but for climbing trees and digging for tasty roots. "Did you know that some of us Velociraptors had feathers just like birds?" Vinnie said proudly, fluffing up his colorful scales.

The young dinosaurs were fascinated. They had never heard such things before. Their journey continued, and they came across various dinosaur footprints. Vinnie taught them how to identify different dinosaurs by their tracks.

As the sun began to set, painting the sky in hues of orange and pink, Vinnie led his new friends to a clearing where they could gaze at the stars. He told them stories about the ancient dinosaurs that roamed the earth long before them, sparking a sense of wonder and curiosity in their hearts.

"Wow, Vinnie, you know so much about dinosaurs!" exclaimed Tara, impressed by Vinnie's knowledge.

Vinnie chuckled softly. "There's always something new to learn, especially about friends who are different from us. Just like how you all learned that a Velociraptor can be friendly!"

The young dinosaurs nodded in agreement, their eyes filled with new understanding and respect for different creatures.

As the night grew deeper, Vinnie knew it was time to head back. He led his new friends safely to their homes, promising to meet them again for more adventures.
From that day on, Vinnie and his friends explored the forest together, learning and sharing. They met other dinosaurs who were surprised to see a friendly Velociraptor, and soon, Vinnie's kindness spread throughout the land.

The forest was filled with laughter and joy as the dinosaurs lived in harmony, understanding and celebrating their differences. And as for Vinnie, he was no longer the misunderstood Velociraptor. He was Vinnie, the friendly Velociraptor, who taught everyone that it's not how you look, but how you are on the inside that truly matters.

And so, in a world where every dinosaur is unique, Vinnie's story reminds us that friendship and kindness are the most wonderful traits of all.

The End.

THE SUN'S SOLAR
SECRETS

Once upon a time, in a cozy little house on Earth, lived a curious young boy named Timmy. Timmy loved to gaze at the stars and dream about space.

One clear night, as he looked up at the sky, he made a wish upon a shooting star. "I wish to visit the sun and learn all its secrets," he whispered.

To Timmy's astonishment, a glowing spaceship appeared in his backyard, shining like a diamond in the moonlight. The door opened, and a friendly robot named Sparky greeted him. "Welcome, Timmy! I'm here to take you on a magical journey to the sun!" Sparky said with a cheerful beep.

Excitedly, Timmy climbed aboard. The spaceship zoomed through the sky, past the twinkling stars, and towards the bright sun. As they traveled, Sparky began to share the sun's solar secrets.

"Did you know, Timmy, that the sun is a giant star at the center of our solar system?" Sparky asked. Timmy's eyes widened with wonder. "It's like a huge ball of fire, giving us light and warmth every day!"

As they got closer, Timmy saw the sun's surface, a dazzling display of golden and orange hues. "Look, those are sunspots," Sparky pointed out. "They are cooler areas on the sun and they look like dark spots."

Timmy was amazed. "Why is the sun so important, Sparky?" he asked.

"The sun is very important for life on Earth," Sparky explained. "It gives us solar energy, which plants use to make food. This energy also keeps our planet warm enough for us to live."

Timmy gazed at the sun, feeling grateful for its warmth and light. Suddenly, he saw bright flashes on the sun's surface. "What's that?" he asked in amazement.

"Those are solar flares, Timmy. They are bursts of energy that can reach far into space," Sparky answered.
Timmy was learning so much and having so much fun! He didn't want the adventure to end. But then he remembered his family and friends back home.

"Sparky, I think it's time for me to go back. I want to tell everyone about the sun's solar secrets!" Timmy said.
"Of course, Timmy," Sparky replied. "Let's head back to Earth."

The spaceship gently descended back to Timmy's backyard. As he stepped out, Timmy felt a warm breeze and looked up at the sun, smiling brightly in the sky.

"Thank you, sun, for all that you do," Timmy whispered.
From that day on, Timmy shared the sun's solar secrets with everyone he met, spreading the wonder and importance of our magnificent sun.

And every night, before he went to sleep, Timmy would look out his window, wave at the stars, and whisper, "Thank you, Sparky, for the amazing adventure."

The End.

THE INTERNATIONAL SPACE STATION

Once upon a time, in the vast, twinkling expanse of space, floated a very special house called the International Space Station (ISS). In this extraordinary house lived a unique family: astronaut Mom, Dad, and their two curious kids, Lily and Max.

The ISS was not like any other house you've seen. It didn't stand on the ground; instead, it orbited our beautiful Earth, high above the clouds. It was like a magic house that could float!
Lily and Max were very excited to live in space. Every morning, they would float out of their sleeping bags, as there was no gravity like on Earth. Instead of walking, they learned to push off walls and glide through the air, which was so much fun!

Their days were filled with amazing adventures. Mom and Dad taught them about the stars and planets. They even had a special window, called the Cupola, where they could see the Earth below, looking like a big, beautiful blue and green marble.

One day, Dad showed Lily and Max how to grow plants in space. They planted tiny seeds in a special space garden. Without soil, the plants grew in a mist filled with nutrients. Lily and Max were amazed to see the plants growing sideways and in circles because, in space, there's no up or down like on Earth.

Mom was a scientist and sometimes conducted experiments, which Lily and Max found fascinating. They learned about how water forms spheres in zero gravity and how different materials behave in space. They even got to help with some of the simpler experiments!

Living on the ISS also meant exercising every day. In space, muscles and bones can get weaker because they're not used as much, so the family had to stay strong and healthy. They had special machines for this, like a space treadmill and a weightlifting machine that used air pressure instead of weights. Exercising in space was different but fun – sometimes Lily and Max would accidentally flip upside down!

One of their favorite activities was talking to children on Earth via video calls. They loved sharing their experiences and what they learned about space. Children from all over the world would ask them questions, and Lily and Max were always eager to answer.

"Is it dark in space?" one child asked during a call.

"Not always," Max replied. "We see the sunrise and sunset many times a day because we orbit the Earth so fast!"

Another asked, "Do you miss Earth?"

Lily smiled and said, "We do, but we also love being here. It's important to learn about space to help us take care of our planet Earth."

The family also had to deal with challenges. Sometimes, they missed things from Earth, like the feel of rain or the sound of birds. But they had each other, and that made everything better. They would often gather in the Cupola, look at the Earth, and talk about their favorite memories from home.

As their time on the ISS was coming to an end, Lily and Max were both happy and sad. They were excited to return to Earth, but they would miss their extraordinary space home.
On their last day, the family packed their belongings. They put on their special space suits and boarded the spacecraft that would take them back to Earth. As the ISS grew smaller and smaller in the window, Lily and Max waved goodbye.

Re-entering Earth's atmosphere was thrilling. The spacecraft shuddered and roared as it traveled through the sky. And then, with a gentle bump, they landed back on Earth.
Stepping out of the spacecraft, Lily and Max felt the fresh air and the warmth of the sun. They were home, but they knew they would always carry a piece of the ISS in their hearts.

Back on Earth, Lily and Max shared their stories and what they had learned about space and the importance of caring for our planet. They knew that one day, they might return to space, but for now, they were happy to be home, surrounded by the beauty of Earth.

And so, the family's incredible adventure in space came to an end, but their journey of discovery and learning would continue, under the wide, endless sky of our wonderful planet.

The End.

THE GOLD RUSH
ADVENTURE

Once upon a time, in the heart of a bustling city, there was a small, cozy library. In this library lived a magical book, shimmering with golden letters on its cover. It was no ordinary book; it was a portal to the past, filled with stories of adventures and wonders. This book was especially loved by two curious children, Emma and Leo.

One sunny afternoon, Emma and Leo were exploring the library, when they stumbled upon the golden book. As they opened it, a whirlwind of golden sparkles enveloped them, and they were whisked away to a different time and place.
They landed softly on the dusty ground of a busy town, filled with people wearing wide-brimmed hats and carrying shovels. The air was buzzing with excitement. "Where are we?" whispered Emma.

"We're in the Gold Rush era!" exclaimed Leo, recognizing the scene from the pictures in the book.

The Gold Rush was a time when people from all over came to find gold. They believed that finding gold would make them rich and fulfill their dreams. The town was alive with miners, merchants, and adventurers, all hoping for a lucky break.

Emma and Leo wandered through the town, marveling at the wooden buildings and horses trotting down the dirt roads. They met a friendly miner named Mr. Thompson, who was about to head to the river to pan for gold. "Would you like to join me?" Mr. Thompson asked with a smile.

Excitedly, Emma and Leo agreed. They followed Mr. Thompson to the river, where he showed them how to use a pan to sift through the river's waters in search of gold.

As they swirled the water in their pans, Mr. Thompson shared stories of the Gold Rush. He told them how it wasn't just about finding gold, but also about the journey and the friendships formed along the way. Many people didn't find gold, but they found something more valuable – a sense of adventure and the joy of trying something new.

Emma and Leo listened, fascinated by the tales of perseverance and hope. They learned that the Gold Rush was more than just a search for riches; it was a part of history that brought people together from different places and changed the course of many lives.

After a while, Leo's pan shimmered with a tiny speck of gold. "I found gold!" he shouted in delight. Emma clapped her hands in excitement. But soon, they realized that the true treasure was the experience and the stories they had heard.

As the sun began to set, Mr. Thompson thanked them for their company and handed them a small vial with the gold speck. "Keep this as a reminder of your adventure and the lessons of the Gold Rush," he said warmly.

Just then, the golden sparkles reappeared, swirling around Emma and Leo. They waved goodbye to Mr. Thompson and found themselves back in the library, holding the vial and the golden book.

The librarian, seeing their amazed expressions, asked, "Did you enjoy your adventure?"

Emma and Leo nodded eagerly, sharing their incredible journey and the lessons they learned about hope, perseverance, and the real treasures in life.

From that day on, the golden book held a special place in their hearts. They realized that adventures could be found not only in faraway places but also in the stories and history of the world.

And so, Emma and Leo often visited the library, reading and learning, always remembering their Gold Rush Adventure and the magical journey that taught them the value of history, friendship, and the joy of discovery.

The End.

THE GREAT BARRIER REEF

Once upon a time, in the vast and sparkling waters of the ocean, there was a magical place called the Great Barrier Reef. This reef was not just any reef;

it was the biggest and most colorful reef in all the seas, home to a wonderful array of creatures big and small.

Our story begins with a little green sea turtle named Timmy. Timmy was not like other turtles; he was curious and adventurous, always eager to explore the wonders of his underwater world. One sunny day, Timmy decided to embark on a journey across the Great Barrier Reef to learn about marine life and the importance of coral reefs.

As Timmy swam, he marveled at the kaleidoscope of colors around him. The coral was like a giant underwater garden, bursting with pinks, purples, yellows, and blues. He saw fish of all shapes and sizes, from tiny neon tetras darting in the water to majestic angelfish gliding gracefully.

Timmy's first friend on his journey was Charlie, a clownfish with bright orange and white stripes. Charlie lived in an anemone, a special kind of plant that protected him from predators. "Hello, Timmy!" Charlie greeted him with a smile. "Welcome to the Great Barrier Reef! Isn't it beautiful?"

"It's amazing!" Timmy exclaimed. "But why are coral reefs important, Charlie?"

"Coral reefs are like the cities of the sea," Charlie explained. "They provide food and shelter for many marine creatures. Without them, many of us wouldn't survive."

As Timmy swam on, he met more friends. There was Sally the starfish, who loved to lounge on the rocks, and Barry the blue tang, who was always busy cleaning the reef. Each creature had a special role in keeping the reef healthy and vibrant.

The next day, Timmy came across a part of the reef that looked different. The colors were faded, and there were fewer fish. He met an old turtle named Oliver, who looked sad. "What happened here, Oliver?" Timmy asked.

"This part of the reef is dying," Oliver said softly. "It's because of pollution and climate change. The water is getting too warm for the coral, and it's losing its color and life."

Timmy felt a pang of sadness. "Is there anything we can do to help?" he asked.

"Yes, there is," Oliver replied. "We must take care of our ocean. Don't throw trash in the water, save energy to reduce climate change, and tell others about the importance of coral reefs. We all have a part to play in protecting our home."

Filled with determination, Timmy continued his journey, sharing Oliver's message with every creature he met. He talked to schools of fish, whispering seahorses, and even a playful pod of dolphins. They all agreed to help protect their beautiful home.

As Timmy's adventure came to an end, he realized that the Great Barrier Reef was more than just a place; it was a community, a family of different creatures living together in harmony. He promised himself that he would always work to protect it and spread the word about its importance.

Timmy swam back to his favorite part of the reef, where the water was clear, and the coral was bright. He knew that with everyone working together, the reef would continue to be a magical, colorful wonderland for generations to come.

And so, the Great Barrier Reef thrived, a testament to the power of unity and care.

The End.

ENCHANTMENT IN THE ELVEN CITY

Once upon a time, in a world far, far away, there was a little boy named Oliver. Oliver was just six years old, and he had a heart full of curiosity and a mind bursting with imagination. Every night before bedtime, he would close his eyes and dream of magical lands, talking animals, and brave adventures.

One sunny morning, while Oliver was playing in his backyard, he heard a soft, tinkling sound. It was like the most beautiful chime he had ever heard. He followed the sound until he found himself standing at the edge of a mysterious forest. The trees in this forest were tall and ancient, their leaves shimmering like emerald jewels.

As Oliver took a hesitant step into the forest, he felt a gentle breeze that carried the sweet scent of flowers and the promise of something magical. The trees seemed to whisper secrets to him, and the path ahead beckoned him forward. With his heart pounding in excitement, Oliver ventured deeper into the forest.

The further he walked, the more enchanted the forest became. Fireflies danced around him, leaving trails of sparkling light, and the flowers seemed to sing with their vibrant colors. Birds with feathers of every hue sang melodious songs from the treetops, as if welcoming him to their world.

After what felt like an eternity, Oliver stumbled upon a clearing bathed in golden light. In the center of the clearing stood a magnificent archway made of vines and flowers. Beyond the archway, he could see an entire city made of crystal and silver, nestled among the treetops.

Oliver gasped in awe as he realized that he had stumbled upon the Elven City, a place of magic and wonder. The city seemed to glow with an inner light, and it was unlike anything he had ever seen in his wildest dreams.

With a sense of adventure burning in his heart, Oliver walked through the archway and into the city. Everywhere he looked, he saw elves with pointed ears, their eyes twinkling with mischief and kindness. They greeted him with warm smiles and welcomed him to their city.
The Elven City was a place of endless enchantment. The buildings were made of crystal and silver, and they sparkled like diamonds in the sunlight.

The streets were paved with golden leaves, and the fountains bubbled with water that shone like liquid gold. Magical creatures roamed freely, from unicorns to talking animals, and the air was filled with the melodious songs of fairies.

Oliver spent his days exploring the Elven City, learning about the wonders of this fantastical world. He met a wise old elf who taught him the secrets of the enchanted forest and the language of the animals. He learned to ride on the back of a friendly dragon and soared high above the city, feeling the wind in his hair and the thrill of adventure in his heart.

In the evenings, Oliver would sit by the shimmering lake and listen to the stories of the elder elves. They told him tales of bravery, friendship, and the magic that lived within each of us. Oliver learned that in the Elven City, anything was possible, and imagination was the key to unlocking its endless wonders.

One day, as Oliver was exploring the city, he came across a beautiful crystal amulet. The amulet seemed to radiate with a special energy, and he knew it was a powerful artifact of the Elven City. The elves told him that the amulet had the power to make any wish come true, but only if the wish was made from the purest heart.

Oliver thought long and hard about his wish. He knew that he could wish for anything in the world, but he also knew that he had found something even more precious than any material possession – a world of magic and imagination. With a smile on his face, Oliver closed his eyes and made his wish: "I wish for the magic of the Elven City to stay alive in my heart forever, so I can share it with others."

As soon as he made his wish, the amulet began to glow brightly and then disappeared, leaving behind a warm feeling in Oliver's heart. The elves cheered and clapped, for they knew that Oliver's wish had come true. The magic of the Elven City would live on in his heart, and he would share it with the world.

With a heart full of gratitude and a spirit full of adventure, Oliver said his farewells to the Elven City. He stepped back through the archway and into his own world, carrying with him the enchantment and wonder of the magical land he had discovered.

From that day forward, Oliver continued to dream of fantastical worlds and magical adventures. He shared his stories with other children, teaching them about the power of imagination and the wonders that could be found within the pages of a book or the depths of their own minds.

And so, the enchantment of the Elven City lived on, not only in Oliver's heart but in the hearts of all the children who listened to his stories. And as long as there were dreamers like Oliver, the magic of the Elven City would never fade away, but continue to inspire generations to come.

The End.

THE PALEONTOLOGIST'S DREAM

Once upon a time, in a land filled with ancient secrets, there lived a young Indian paleontologist named Aarav. Aarav was not like other kids his age; instead of playing with toys, he spent his days reading about dinosaurs, their enormous sizes, and their mysterious lives. His room was filled with dinosaur posters, fossils he had collected, and books about these magnificent creatures.

One sunny morning, Aarav received an exciting invitation from the National Museum of Natural History. They wanted him to join a special expedition to dig for dinosaur fossils in the Thar Desert. Aarav's heart leaped with joy! He had always dreamed of discovering a new dinosaur species, and now he might have the chance.

The next day, Aarav, equipped with his trusty digging tools and a big hat to shield him from the sun, set off on his adventure. The desert was vast and golden, with sand dunes rolling like waves in a sandy sea. The team worked under the scorching sun, digging carefully, sifting through sand and stone.

Days passed with no sign of a dinosaur fossil. But Aarav didn't lose hope. He remembered what his favorite book said: "Paleontology requires patience, for the secrets of the past are deeply buried." So, he dug on, fueled by his passion and dreams.

Then, on the seventh day, Aarav's shovel hit something hard. He brushed away the sand gently, and to his amazement, he uncovered a giant bone, unlike any he had seen in books. It was the thigh bone of a dinosaur, but it was much larger and had a unique shape.

Excitement buzzed through the air as the team gathered around Aarav's discovery. They worked together to unearth more bones. Slowly, the skeleton of a massive dinosaur, never seen before, emerged from the sands.

Aarav named the dinosaur "Bharatasaurus," meaning 'The Giant Lizard from India.' It was a herbivore, as big as a bus, with long legs for running fast and a long neck to reach the highest tree leaves. Bharatasaurus had a unique pattern of bony plates along its back, which made it different from all other known dinosaurs.

The discovery of Bharatasaurus made headlines around the world. Aarav became known as the boy who discovered a new dinosaur. The National Museum of Natural History set up a special exhibit with Bharatasaurus, and Aarav was invited to talk about his discovery to kids who visited the museum.

Aarav told them about the importance of following their dreams and never giving up, just like he had. He explained how every dinosaur, big or small, had its role in the prehistoric world, just like every one of us has a unique place in the world today.

The kids listened with wide eyes, imagining the giant Bharatasaurus roaming the ancient lands of India. Aarav's story inspired them to learn more about dinosaurs and the wonders of the past.

And so, Aarav's dream became a story of inspiration, showing that even the wildest dreams could come true with passion, patience, and perseverance. The Paleontologist's Dream was not just about discovering a new dinosaur; it was about igniting the flame of curiosity and adventure in the hearts of all who heard it.

From that day on, Aarav continued to explore and study, always in search of new discoveries, and always ready to share the magic of the ancient world with others. And somewhere, in the vast, golden sands of the Thar Desert, the secrets of the past waited, ready to be uncovered by the next dreamer.

The End.

GALACTIC OLYMPICS

Once upon a time, in the vast, twinkling expanse of the universe, there was a special event that brought together beings from all corners of the galaxies. This event was known as the Galactic Olympics, a grand sports festival celebrating teamwork, friendship, and the wondrous diversity of life across the stars.

In a small, blue-green planet called Earth, a young girl named Lily gazed up at the night sky, her eyes sparkling with dreams of distant worlds. One starry night, as she peered through her telescope, a shimmering light descended from the heavens. It was a colorful, gleaming spacecraft, and out stepped Zara, a friendly alien from the planet Glorbon.

Zara came with an exciting invitation for Lily and her friends: to join the Galactic Olympics! With a burst of joy and excitement, Lily and her friends, Max, Aisha, and Pablo, boarded the spacecraft. They zoomed past comets, nebulas, and planets, meeting new friends from all across the universe.

The Olympic village was a sight to behold, a swirling constellation of habitats and arenas floating in space. Creatures of all shapes and sizes, colors and textures, greeted them with warm smiles and curious glances. There were the tall, leafy beings from Floranox, the twinkling, crystal-like creatures from Crystallia, and the bubbly, floating orbs from Gaseon.

The first event was Space Soccer, a game played in zero gravity. Lily and her friends, joined by their new alien companions, formed a team. They learned to move and pass the ball in the weightlessness of space, laughing as they somersaulted and twirled. Despite the challenge, they worked together, communicating and supporting each other.

Next was the Asteroid Race, a thrilling dash through a field of gently floating asteroids. Max, with his love for speed, was eager to participate. Guided by his new friend, a speedy Floranox named Fern, Max learned the importance of patience and careful navigation. Together, they zipped and dodged, learning from each other's strengths.

The third event was the Cosmic Puzzle, a game of logic and teamwork. Aisha, with her sharp mind and keen eye for detail, took the lead. Teamed with a Crystallian named Crystal, they solved intricate puzzles that required them to think in new and creative ways. The puzzles weren't just challenges; they were stories of different planets and cultures, teaching them about the vast and varied tapestry of the universe.

Finally, there was the Intergalactic Relay, a race that combined all the skills they had learned. Pablo, with his warm heart and inclusive spirit, reminded everyone that winning wasn't everything; what mattered most was the fun and friendship they shared. As they passed the baton from tentacle to leaf, to paw, to hand, they realized that their differences made them stronger together.

At the end of the Galactic Olympics, there was a grand celebration. Lights danced in the sky, and music from a thousand worlds filled the air. Lily and her friends, surrounded by their new intergalactic friends, felt a profound sense of unity and wonder.

As they returned to Earth, waving goodbye to their new friends, Lily and her friends knew they would always cherish these memories. They had not only participated in the Galactic Olympics but had also learned valuable lessons about teamwork, diversity, and the beauty of friendship that spans across the stars.

And every time they looked up at the night sky, they remembered their incredible adventure and the friends they had made, knowing that somewhere out there, in the vast, beautiful universe, those friends were looking back at them.

The End.

THE FAMILY TREE ADVENTURE

Once upon a time in a cozy little town, there was a curious young boy named Max. Max loved adventures and had a vivid imagination. He lived with his mom, dad, and his little sister Lily in a house filled with laughter and love. One sunny afternoon, Max found an old, dusty book in the attic. It was titled "Our Family Tree." Intrigued, Max gathered his family in the living room.

"Look what I found!" Max exclaimed, holding the book high. His parents smiled, knowing it was time to share their family's history.

he book was magical. With each page turn, Max and his family were transported to different times and places, meeting their ancestors. Their first stop was a farm where they met Great-Grandpa Joe, a brave and kind farmer who loved his land and animals. Max and Lily helped him feed the chickens, and they listened to his stories about the farm passed down through generations.

Next, they traveled to a bustling city where they met Great-Great-Grandma Mabel, an accomplished baker known for her delicious pies. In her cozy bakery, she taught Max and Lily how to bake apple pies, filling the air with sweet aromas.

The adventure continued as they met more ancestors, each with a unique story. There was Aunt Sophia, a talented musician; Uncle Leo, a courageous firefighter; and many more. With each visit, Max and Lily learned about their ancestors' struggles, achievements, and dreams.

One evening, as they turned the last page, they found themselves back in their living room. Max and Lily were amazed by the journey they had just experienced. Their parents smiled, seeing their children's eyes filled with wonder.

"Each of our ancestors has contributed to who we are today," their mom explained. "They have passed down more than just their looks and talents. They have given us values, strength, and love."

Max and Lily understood that their family was like a tree. Just as a tree grows branches, their family had grown through generations. Each ancestor was like a branch, strong and unique, connected to the same roots.

The next day at school, Max and Lily couldn't wait to share their adventure. They told their friends about the magical book and the ancestors they met. Their friends were fascinated and wanted to learn about their own families.

That night, Max and Lily decided to add their own stories to the family tree book. They drew pictures and wrote about their dreams and what they loved. They knew that one day, their descendants would read about them and continue the family tree adventure.

As they grew up, Max and Lily often revisited the book, adding new stories and photos. The book became a treasure, filled with the history and love of generations.

Years later, Max and Lily, now adults, passed the family tree book to their own children. They watched with joy as their children's eyes sparkled with curiosity, ready to embark on their own family tree adventure.

And so, the story of their family continued, each generation adding its own chapter to the ever-growing tree. Max and Lily knew that as long as their family's stories were shared, the roots of their family tree would remain strong, and their bond would never be broken.
The End.

KNIGHTS OF THE ROUND TABLE

Once upon a time, in a land filled with rolling hills and sparkling rivers, there stood a magnificent castle. This castle was home to the bravest and kindest knights in all the land - the Knights of the Round Table.

In the heart of the castle, there was a grand room with a huge round table. It was not just any table, but a special one where all the knights would gather to discuss important matters and plan their adventures. Each knight had his own seat at the table, and at the head sat the wisest and most noble of them all, King Arthur.

One sunny morning, King Arthur called his knights to the Round Table. "My dear knights," he said, "I have heard of a distant village that needs our help. They are being troubled by a mischievous dragon who loves to play tricks on them. We must go and ensure the safety of the village."

The knights, wearing their shining armor and colorful capes, mounted their trusty horses. They rode through the lush green forests, over sparkling streams, and across wide open fields. Along the way, they saw rabbits hopping in the meadows and birds singing in the trees.

As they neared the village, they saw the dragon. But to their surprise, the dragon was not scary at all! He was a playful creature with bright green scales and gentle eyes. The knights soon realized that the dragon was just lonely and wanted friends to play with.

The knights had an idea. They invited the dragon to the castle and introduced him to the villagers. Together, they organized a grand feast. There was delicious food, music, and dancing. The dragon entertained everyone with his amazing ability to make colorful flames and smoke rings.

The knights taught the villagers and the dragon about kindness, sharing, and being good friends. The dragon promised to be gentle and help the village instead of causing trouble. The villagers, in turn, welcomed the dragon into their community.

As the sun set, the knights rode back to their castle, their hearts full of joy. They had not only helped the village but also made a new friend. Back at the Round Table, they shared their adventure with King Arthur, who was very proud of them.

From that day on, the dragon would often visit the castle. He would play with the knights and even help them on their adventures. The Knights of the Round Table had shown everyone that even the most unexpected friendships could be the most magical.

And so, the kingdom was filled with laughter, joy, and harmony, all thanks to the brave and kind Knights of the Round Table and their new dragon friend.

The End.

THANK YOU

This is a note for you, the reader. I want to take a moment to thank you for reading these short stories.

As a token of our appreciation, here is a QR code you can redeem at www.bedtimenewsletter.com to receive a free month of daily bedtime stories.

ABOUT THE AUTHOR

Marc Sala López

Marc and his family were a bit disappointed and frustrated with story time. One night, after a long time deciding what to read, Marc thought "I wish I got stories daily delivered to me everyday, it would make story time so much easier." That's how BedtimeNewsletter.com was born, and thus, this book.

BOOKS BY THIS AUTHOR

30 Bedtime Stories For 30 Different Nights Vol. 2

Welcome back to the magical world of dreams and adventures with "30 Bedtime Stories for 30 Different Nights Vol. 2," the eagerly awaited sequel that promises even more enchanting bedtime tales for children. Each story, crafted for a delightful 5-minute read, is a treasure chest of wonders.

30 Bedtime Stories For 30 Different Nights Vol. 3

Embark on a journey through the pages of "30 Bedtime Stories for 30 Different Nights Vol. 3," the latest installment in the cherished series that has lulled countless children to sleep with tales of wonder, adventure, and discovery. Each story unfolds in just five minutes, making them the perfect length for a cozy bedtime reading session.

Printed in Great Britain
by Amazon

40196578R00066